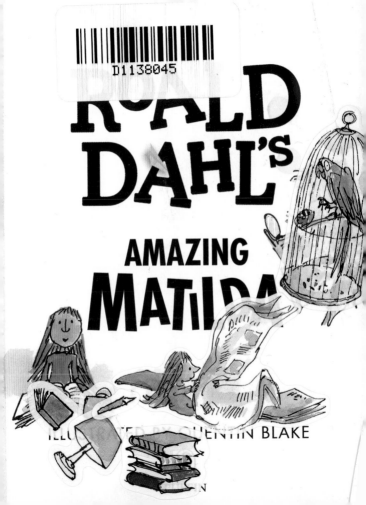

ROALD DAHL'S

AMAZING MATILDA

ILLUSTRATED BY QUENTIN BLAKE

PUFFIN BOOKS

UK | USA | Canada | Ireland | Australia
India | New Zealand | South Africa

Puffin Books is part of the Penguin Random House group of companies
whose addresses can be found at global.penguinrandomhouse.com.

www.penguin.co.uk   www.puffin.co.uk   www.ladybird.co.uk

Penguin
Random House
UK

Made for McDonald's 2017
001

Matilda: first published by Jonathan Cape 1988
Published in paperback by Puffin Books

Printed in China
THH
A CIP catalogue record for this book is available from the British Library

ISBN: 978-0-141-38638-6

The National Literacy Trust is a registered charity no. 1116260 and a company limited
by guarantee no. 5836486 registered in England and Wales and a registered charity in
Scotland no. SC042944. Registered address: 68 South Lambeth Road, London SW8 1RL.
National Literacy Trust logo and reading tips copyright © National Literacy Trust, 2017
www.literacytrust.org.uk/donate

Date code: A7F

Meet
AMAZING
MATiLDA!

She may be **SMALL**, but her
mind can do **BRILLIANT** things!

Turn the page to find out what
CLEVER TRICKS she has
up her sleeve.

Turn to the
back of your book
for **STICKERS**
and a handy
BOOKMARK

SEARCH and **FIND!**

Can you **SPOT THIS CHARACTER** in the book?

WHO IS HE?

THE READER OF BOOKS

It's a funny thing about mothers and fathers. Even when their own child is the most disgusting little blister you could ever imagine, they still think that he or she is wonderful.

Some parents go further. They become so blinded by adoration they manage to convince themselves their child has qualities of genius.

Occasionally one comes across parents who take the opposite line, who show no interest at all in their children, and these of course are far worse than the doting ones. Mr and Mrs Wormwood were two such parents. They had a son called Michael and a daughter called Matilda, and the parents looked upon Matilda in

particular as nothing more than a scab.
A scab is something you have to put
up with until the time comes when you
can pick it off and flick it away. Mr
and Mrs Wormwood looked forward
enormously to the time when they
could pick their little daughter off and
flick her away, preferably into the next

county or even further than that.

It is bad enough when parents treat *ordinary* children as though they were scabs and bunions, but it becomes somehow a lot worse when the child in question is *extra*-ordinary, and by that I mean sensitive and brilliant. Matilda was both of these things, but above all she was brilliant. Her mind was so nimble and she was so quick to learn that her ability should

Colour me in!

have been obvious even to the most half-witted of parents. But Mr and Mrs Wormwood were both so gormless and so wrapped up in their own silly little lives that they failed to notice anything unusual about their daughter.

Matilda's brother Michael was a perfectly normal boy, but the sister, as I said, was something to make your eyes pop. By the age of *one and a half* her speech was perfect and she knew as many words as most grown-ups. The parents, instead of applauding her,

called her a noisy chatterbox and told
her sharply that small girls should be
seen and not heard.

By the time she was *three*, Matilda
had taught herself to read by studying
newspapers and magazines that lay
around the house. At the age of *four*,
she could read fast and well and
she naturally began hankering after
books. The only book
in the whole of this

enlightened household was something called *Easy Cooking* belonging to her mother, and when she had read this from cover to cover and had learnt all the recipes by heart, she decided she wanted something more interesting.

'Daddy,' she said, 'do you think you could buy me a book?'

'What's wrong with the telly, for heaven's sake?' he said. 'We've got a lovely telly with a twelve-inch screen and now you come asking for a book! You're getting spoiled, my girl!'

Nearly every weekday afternoon Matilda was left alone in the house. Her brother (five years older than her) went to school. Her father went to work and her mother went out playing bingo in a town eight miles away. On the afternoon of the day when her father had refused to buy her a book, Matilda

 set out all by
herself to walk
to the public
library in the
village. When
she arrived, she
introduced herself to the librarian,
Mrs Phelps. She asked if she might sit
awhile and read a book. Mrs Phelps,
slightly taken aback at the arrival of
such a tiny girl unaccompanied by a
parent, nevertheless told her she was
very welcome.

'Where are the children's books please?' Matilda asked.

'They're over there on those lower shelves,' Mrs Phelps told her. 'Would you like me to help you find a nice one with lots of pictures in it?'

'No, thank you,' Matilda said. 'I'm sure I can manage.'

From then on, every afternoon, as soon as her mother had left for bingo, Matilda would toddle down to the library. The walk took only ten minutes and this allowed her two glorious

hours sitting quietly
by herself in a cosy
corner devouring
one book after
another. When she
had read every single
children's book in
the place, she started
wandering round in
search of something else.

Mrs Phelps, who had been watching
her with fascination for the past few
weeks, now got up from her desk and

went over to her. 'Can I help you, Matilda?' she asked.

'I'm wondering what to read next,' Matilda said. 'I've finished all the children's books.'

'You mean you've looked at the pictures?'

'Yes, but I've read the books as well.'

Mrs Phelps looked down at Matilda from her great height and Matilda looked right back up at her.

Mrs Phelps was stunned. 'Exactly how old are you, Matilda?' she asked.

'Four years and three months,' Matilda said.

Mrs Phelps was more stunned than ever, but she had the sense not to show it. 'What sort of a book would you like to read next?' she asked.

Matilda said, 'I would like a really good one

that grown-ups read. A famous one. I don't know any names.'

Mrs Phelps looked along the shelves, taking her time. 'Try this,' she said at last. 'It's very famous and very good. If it's too long for you, just let me know and I'll find something shorter and a bit easier.'

'*Great Expectations*,' Matilda read, 'by Charles Dickens. I'd love to try it.'

I must be mad, Mrs Phelps told herself, but to Matilda she said, 'Of course you may try it.'

OFF TO THE LIBRARY

Help Matilda navigate her way from her house to Mrs Phelps in the library.

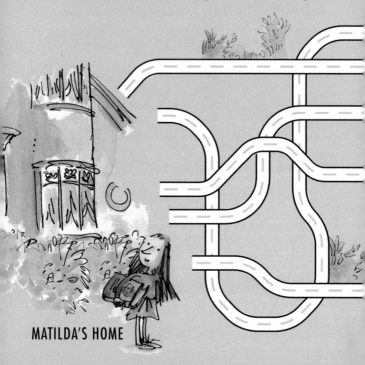

MATILDA'S HOME

LIBRARY

Answer on page 62

MATILDA'S TRAVELS

Over the next few afternoons
Mrs Phelps could hardly take her
eyes from the small girl sitting for
hour after hour in the big armchair
at the far end of the room with the
book on her lap. It was necessary
to rest it on the lap because it was
too heavy for her to hold up, which
meant she had to sit leaning forward
in order to read. And a strange
sight it was, this tiny dark-haired
person sitting there with her feet

nowhere near touching the floor,
totally absorbed in the wonderful
adventures of Pip and old Miss
Havisham and her cobwebbed
house and by the spell of magic that
Dickens the great story-teller had
woven with
his words.
The only
movement
from the
reader was
the lifting

of the hand every now and then to turn over a page, and Mrs Phelps always felt sad when the time came for her to cross the floor and say, 'It's ten to five, Matilda.'

During the first week of Matilda's visits Mrs Phelps had said to her, 'Does your mother walk you down here every day and then take you home?'

'My mother goes to Aylesbury every afternoon to

play bingo,' Matilda had said. 'She doesn't know I come here.'

'But that's surely not right,' Mrs Phelps said. 'I think you'd better ask her.'

'She doesn't really care what I do,' Matilda said a little sadly.

Mrs Phelps was concerned about the child's safety on the walk through the fairly busy village High Street and the crossing of the road, but she decided not to interfere.

'Did you know,' Mrs Phelps said one day, 'that public libraries like this allow you to borrow books and take them home?'

'I didn't know that,' Matilda said. 'Could *I* do it?'

'Of course,' Mrs Phelps said. 'When you have chosen the book you want, bring it to me so I can make a note of it and it's yours for two weeks. You can take more than one if you wish.'

From then on, Matilda would visit the library only once a week in order to take out new books and return the old ones. Her own small bedroom now became her reading-room and there she would sit and read most afternoons, often with a mug of hot chocolate beside her. It was pleasant to take a hot drink up to her room and have it beside her as she sat in her silent room reading in the empty house in the afternoons.

The books transported her into
new worlds and introduced her to
amazing people who lived exciting
lives. She went on olden-day sailing
ships with Joseph Conrad. She went
to Africa with Ernest Hemingway
and to India with Rudyard Kipling.
She travelled all over the world while
sitting in her little room in
an English village.

BOREDOM BUSTER

Matilda is waiting for her mother to return from bingo – again! Help her pass the time by designing and colouring in the cover of her new book.

ARITHMETIC

Matilda longed for her parents to be good and loving and understanding and honourable and intelligent. The fact that they were none of these things was something she had to put up with. It was not easy to do so.

Being very small and very young, the only power Matilda had over anyone in her family was brain-power. For sheer cleverness she could run rings around them all. But the fact remained that any five-year-old girl in any family was

always obliged to do as she was told,
however asinine the orders might be.
Thus she was always forced to eat
her evening meals out of TV-dinner-
trays in front of the dreaded box. She
always had to stay alone
on weekday afternoons,
and whenever
she was told
to shut up,
she had
to shut
up.

One evening, Mr Wormwood had
just returned from work, where he was
a used car salesman. Matilda and her
brother were sitting quietly on the sofa
waiting for their mother to bring in the
TV dinners on a tray. The television
had not yet been switched on.

In came Mr Wormwood
in a loud check suit
and a yellow tie. The
appalling broad
orange-
and-green

check of the jacket and trousers almost blinded the onlooker. He sat down in an armchair and rubbed his hands together and addressed his son in a loud voice. 'Well, my boy,' he said, 'your father's had a most successful day. He is a lot richer tonight than he was this morning. He has sold no less than five cars, each one at a tidy profit. Sawdust in the gear-boxes, the electric drill on the speedometer cables, a splash of paint here and there and a few other clever little tricks and the idiots were all falling over themselves to buy.'

He fished a bit of paper from his pocket and studied it. 'Listen, boy,' he said, addressing the son and ignoring Matilda, 'seeing as you'll be going into this business with me one day, you've got to know how to add up the profits you make at the end of each day. Go and get yourself a pad and a pencil and let's see how clever you are.'

The son obediently left the room and returned with the writing materials.

'Write down these figures,' the father

said, reading from his bit of paper. 'Car number one was bought by me for two hundred and seventy-eight pounds and sold for one thousand, four hundred and twenty-five. Got that?'

The ten-year-old boy wrote the two separate amounts down slowly and carefully.

Colour me in!

'Car number two,' the father went on, 'cost me one hundred and eighteen pounds and sold for seven hundred and sixty. Got it?'

'Yes, Dad,' the son said. 'I've got that.'

'Car number three cost one hundred and eleven pounds and sold for nine hundred and ninety-nine pounds and fifty pence. Car number four cost eighty-six pounds – a real wreck that was – and sold for six hundred and ninety-nine pounds fifty.'

'Not too fast,' the son said, writing the numbers down. 'Right. I've got it.'

'Car number five cost six hundred and thirty-seven pounds and sold for sixteen hundred and forty-nine fifty. You got all those figures written down, son?'

'Yes, Daddy,' the boy said, crouching over his pad and carefully writing.

'Very well,' the father said. 'Now work out the profit I made on each of the five cars and add up the total. Then you'll be able to tell me how much money your rather brilliant father made altogether today.'

'That's a lot of sums,' the boy said.

'Of course it's a lot of sums,' the father answered. 'But when you're in big business like I am, you've got to be hot stuff at arithmetic. I've practically got a computer inside my head. It took me less than ten minutes to work the whole thing out.'

'You mean you did it in your head, Dad?' the son asked, goggling.

'Well, not exactly,' the father said. 'Nobody could do that. But it didn't take me long. When you're finished, tell me what you think my profit was for the day. I've got the final total written down here and I'll tell you if you're right.'

Matilda said quietly, 'Dad, you made exactly four thousand, three hundred and three pounds and fifty pence altogether.'

'Shut up,' the father said. 'Stop guessing and trying to be clever.'

'Look at your answer, Dad,' Matilda said gently. 'If you've done it right it ought to be four thousand, three hundred and three pounds and fifty pence. Is that what you've got, Dad?'

The father glanced down at the paper in his hand. He seemed to stiffen. He became very quiet.

There was a silence. Then he said, 'Say that again.'

'Four thousand, three hundred and three pounds fifty,' Matilda said.

There was another silence. The father's face was beginning to go dark red.

'I'm sure it's right,' Matilda said.

'You ... you little cheat!' the father suddenly shouted, pointing at her with his finger. 'You looked at my bit of paper! You read it off from what I've got written here!'

'Daddy, I'm the other side of the

room,' Matilda said. 'How could I possibly see it?'

'Don't give me that rubbish!' the father shouted. 'Of course you looked! You must have looked! No one in the world could give the right answer just like that, especially a girl! You're a little cheat, madam, that's what you are! A cheat and a liar!'

PAY ATTENTION!

Matilda is brilliant at problem-solving.
Can you help her solve this puzzle and
spot five differences between these
two pictures of Mr Wormwood?

Answers on page 62

THE PLATINUM-BLOND MAN

There was no doubt in Matilda's mind
that this latest display of foulness by
her father deserved severe punishment,
and as she sat eating awful fried fish
and fried chips and ignoring the
television, her brain went to work on
various possibilities. By the time she
went up to bed her mind was made up.

The next morning she got up early
and went into the bathroom
and locked the door. Mrs
Wormwood's hair was

dyed a brilliant platinum blonde, very
much the same glistening silvery colour
as a female tightrope-walker's tights in
a circus. The big dyeing job was done
twice a year at the hairdresser's, but
every month or so in between, Mrs
Wormwood used to freshen it up by
giving it a rinse in the washbasin with
something called PLATINUM BLONDE
HAIR-DYE EXTRA STRONG. This also
served to dye the nasty brown hairs
that kept growing from the roots
underneath. The bottle of PLATINUM

BLONDE HAIR-DYE EXTRA STRONG was kept in the cupboard in the bathroom, and underneath the title on the label were written the words *Caution, this is peroxide. Keep away from children.* Matilda had read it many times with fascination.

Matilda's father had a fine crop of black hair which he parted in the middle and of which he was exceedingly proud. He kept his hair looking bright and strong, or so he thought, by rubbing into it every morning large quantities of a lotion called OIL OF VIOLETS HAIR TONIC.

A bottle of this smelly purple mixture always stood on the shelf above the sink in the bathroom alongside all the toothbrushes, and a very vigorous scalp massage with OIL OF VIOLETS took place daily after shaving was completed. This hair and scalp massage was always accompanied by loud masculine grunts and heavy breathing and gasps of 'Ahhh, that's

better! That's the stuff! Rub it right into the roots!' which could be clearly heard by Matilda in her bedroom across the corridor.

Now, in the early morning privacy of the bathroom, Matilda unscrewed the cap of her father's OIL OF VIOLETS and tipped three-quarters of the contents down the drain. Then she filled the bottle up with her mother's PLATINUM BLONDE HAIR-DYE EXTRA STRONG. She carefully left enough of her father's original hair tonic in the bottle so that when she gave it a good shake the whole thing still looked reasonably purple. She then replaced the bottle on the shelf above the sink, taking care to put her mother's bottle back in the cupboard. So far so good.

At breakfast time Matilda sat quietly at the dining-room table eating her cornflakes. Her brother sat opposite her with his back to the door devouring hunks of bread smothered with a mixture of peanut-butter and strawberry jam. The mother was just out of sight around the corner in the kitchen making Mr Wormwood's breakfast which always had to be two fried eggs on fried bread with three pork sausages and three strips of bacon and some fried tomatoes.

At this point Mr Wormwood came noisily into the room. He was incapable of entering any room quietly, especially at breakfast time. On this occasion he strode in and slapped his son on the

back and shouted, 'Well, my boy, your
father feels he's in for another great
money-making day today at the garage!
I've got a few little beauties I'm going to
flog to the idiots this morning. Where's
my breakfast?'

'It's coming, treasure,' Mrs
Wormwood called from the kitchen.

Matilda kept her face bent low
over her cornflakes. She didn't dare
look up. In the first place she wasn't
at all sure what she was going to see.
And secondly, if she did see what she

thought she was going to see, she wouldn't trust herself to keep a straight face. The son was looking directly ahead out of the window stuffing himself with bread and peanut-butter and strawberry jam.

The father was just moving round to sit at the head of the table when the mother came sweeping out from the kitchen carrying a huge plate piled high with eggs and sausages and bacon and tomatoes. She looked up. She caught sight of her husband. She stopped dead. Then she let out a scream that seemed to lift her right up into the air and she dropped the plate with a crash and a splash on to the floor. Everyone jumped, including Mr Wormwood.

'What the heck's the matter with you, woman?' he shouted. 'Look at the mess you've made on the carpet!'

'Your *hair*!' the mother was shrieking, pointing a quivering finger at her husband. 'Look at your *hair*!

What've you done to your *hair*?'

'What's wrong with my hair, for heaven's sake?' he said.

'Oh my gawd, Dad, what've you done to your hair?' the son shouted.

A splendid noisy scene was building up nicely in the breakfast room.

Matilda said nothing. She simply sat there admiring the wonderful effect of her own handiwork. Mr Wormwood's fine crop of black hair was now a dirty silver, the colour this time of a tightrope-walker's tights that had not been washed for the entire circus season.

'You've . . . you've . . . you've *dyed* it!' shrieked the mother. 'Why did you do it, you fool! It looks absolutely frightful! It looks horrendous! You look like a freak!'

'What the blazes are you all talking about?' the father yelled, putting both hands to his hair. 'I most certainly have not dyed it! What d'you mean I've dyed it? What's happened to it? Or is this some sort of a stupid joke?' His face was turning pale green, the colour of sour apples.

'You *must* have dyed it, Dad,' the son said. 'It's the same colour as Mum's, only much dirtier-looking.'

'Of course he's dyed it!' the mother cried. 'It can't change colour all by itself! What on earth were you trying to do, make yourself look handsome or something? You look like someone's grandmother gone wrong!'

'Get me a mirror!' the father yelled. 'Don't just stand there shrieking at me!

Get me a mirror!'

The mother's handbag lay on a chair at the other end of the table. She opened the bag and got out a powder compact that had a small round mirror on the inside of the lid. She opened the compact and handed it to her husband. He grabbed it and held it before his face and in doing so spilled most of the powder all over the front of his fancy tweed jacket.

'Oh my gawd!'

yelled the father, staring into the little mirror. 'What's happened to me! I look terrible! I look just like *you* gone wrong! I can't go down to the garage and sell cars like this! How did it happen?' He stared round the room, first at the mother, then at the son, then at Matilda. 'How *could* it have happened?' he yelled.

'I imagine, Daddy,' Matilda said quietly, 'that you weren't looking very hard and you simply took Mummy's

bottle of hair stuff off the shelf

instead of your own.'

'*Of course* that's what happened!' the mother cried. 'Well really, Harry, how stupid can you get? Why didn't you read the label before you started splashing the stuff all over you! Mine's *terribly* strong. I'm only meant to use one tablespoon of it in a whole basin of water and you've gone and put it all over your head neat! It'll probably take all your hair off in the end! Is your scalp beginning to burn, dear?'

'You mean I'm going to lose all my

hair?' the husband yelled.

'I think you will,' the mother said.
'Peroxide is a very powerful chemical.
It's what they put down the lavatory
to disinfect the pan, only they give it
another name. Even diluted like I use
it, it makes a good deal of *my* hair fall
out, so goodness knows what's going
to happen to you. I'm surprised it
didn't take the whole of the top
of your head off!'

'What shall I do?' wailed the
father. 'Tell me quick what to

do before it starts falling out!'

Matilda said, 'I'd give it a good wash, Dad, if I were you, with soap and water. But you'll have to hurry.'

'Will that change the colour back?' the father asked anxiously.

'Of course it won't, you twit,' the mother said.

'Then what do I do? I can't go around looking like this for ever!'

'You'll have to have it dyed black,' the mother said. 'But wash it first or there won't be any there to dye.'

'Right!' the father shouted, springing into action. 'Get me an appointment with your hairdresser this instant for a hair-dyeing job! Tell them it's an emergency! They've got to boot someone else off their list! I'm going upstairs to wash it now!' With that the man dashed out of the room and Mrs Wormwood, sighing deeply, went to the telephone to call the beauty parlour.

WORDSEARCH

Matilda is a brilliant reader.
Can you find these words from her
own story in the wordsearch below?

TRICK
CLEVER
MATHS
PLATINUM
PARENTS
BOOKS

T	A	M	B	O	O	K	S
L	V	T	S	O	T	P	T
S	T	R	T	A	O	T	N
H	O	I	P	R	T	L	E
T	Q	C	L	E	V	E	R
A	V	K	T	S	T	T	A
M	U	N	I	T	A	L	P
T	O	O	R	S	V	K	S

Answers on page 62

Use your stickers to brighten up Matilda's room!

ANSWERS

SEARCH AND FIND

The character shown is Matilda's brother, Michael.

PP.16–17: OFF TO THE LIBRARY

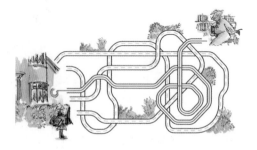

P.39: PAY ATTENTION!

P.59: WORDSEARCH

T	A	M	B	O	O	K	S
L	V	T	S	O	T	P	T
S	T	R	T	A	O	T	N
H	O	I	P	R	T	L	E
T	Q	C	L	E	V	E	R
A	V	K	T	S	T	T	A
M	U	N	I	T	A	L	P
T	O	O	R	S	V	K	S